Love

Jesus

Love Jesus

Katherine Michelle Woods

Kawoo Book Publishing
Chicago, Illinois

Love Jesus

Published by
Kawoo Book Publishing
Chicago, Illinois
kawoo30645@yahoo.com

Katherine Michelle Woods, Publisher / Editorial Director
Yvonne Rose/QualityPress.info, Book Packager

ALL RIGHTS RESERVED

Copyright © 2024 by Katherine Michelle Woods
ISBN #: 979-8-8693-5224-8
Library of Congress Control Number: 2024909065

Acknowledgements

I especially want to thank my daughter, Dr. Susan Gaffney, my brother, Michael Griffin, for their editing assistance, and Marc Moran for providing the front cover graphic. May God bless you and keep you. I pray you will enjoy my book.

Contents

Preface

I am Katherine and I am a Shaliach. Shaliach is a Hebrew word meaning messenger. My mission is to travel all over the world and to say two words to specific people. If they open their hearts and accept Jesus as their Lord and Savior, they will be saved. If they do not accept Jesus, they will be lost.

It all began when I was praying one night. I was kneeling when suddenly, and I mean suddenly, in the blink of an eye, I was whisked away into the night sky. My arms were outstretched before me the way Superman is usually depicted in the movies. I loved it. I found myself in the cockpit of an airplane where the pilot and copilot were talking. They did not see me; I was invisible to them. I said, "Love Jesus." The pilot heard me, but the copilot did not hear me. The pilot stopped in mid-sentence and asked the copilot whether he heard someone say, "Love Jesus." Shaking his head, the copilot responded with a no. I was so glad they didn't see me because I looked horrible with my hair rollers and my nightgown and bed jacket not matching. This was so much fun, although I didn't know what my actual assignment would entail.

Before I could even think about what had just happened, I was flying in a beautiful star-filled sky. I found myself in a kitchen where a family was about to eat dinner: a father, a mother, and two young children. I said to the mother, Love Jesus. The mother heard me, and the six-year-old little girl saw me. I motioned for her not to acknowledge my presence. The little girl giggled and nodded in agreement. The mother glanced around the kitchen, looking confused. After this encounter, my trial run ended, and I found myself kneeling by my bed back at home. I kept thanking Jesus for my supernatural adventure. I made one request of Jesus that I would be allowed to dress appropriately, just in case someone happened to see me. The Lord Jesus allowed me to dress in the fashion my assignment dictated.

Destroyer

The next time I was transported to another location, I wore military fatigues. My clothing was green camouflage with an insignia on the sleeve written in another language, maybe Arabic. There were fifteen of us riding in three Humvees. I was the only woman. Jesus told me that I was to say, "Love Jesus."

The group's leader was Bashir; his name means one who brings good news. I was sure he was not about to deliver good news to anyone. He rode resolutely, determined to kill, maim, and destroy. Bashir wanted to rid the world of infidels who did not believe in his god. They carried dark flags, machetes, assault weapons, and drugs. I thought drugs were forbidden in their religion. Who were these people, and what did they intend to do? I said to Bashir, "Love Jesus." He looked directly at me and said, "Just who the Hell are you?" When he looked around again, I was gone. Bashir was visibly upset. His men began to mumble about hearing someone say, "Love Jesus." Bashir got out of the Humvee and looked all around. Seeing no one, he got back into his vehicle.

The Lord Jesus spoke to him. "Bashir, you shall love the Lord your God with all your soul, might, and strength and love your neighbor as yourself. I was with you when your father threw your pregnant mother on the ground because a midwife told him your mother was having a girl. Your father left you and your mother on a desolate road, hoping you would both die. I sent that stranger in that old pickup truck. He helped your mother deliver you and told your father that you were a boy instead of a girl. You are to help the villagers build a barn and a silo because their harvest will be plentiful. I have blessed them. No one can curse what I have blessed. They are Christians, and they are expecting you. You still have a choice. If you decide to follow your original plan, you will die. If you follow the path I set before you, you will live and thrive."

Bashir answered the Lord and asked what the Lord would have him to do. Bashir reminded me of the Apostle Paul on the road to Damascus. Bashir stopped driving, exited his Humvee, prostrated himself on the ground, and worshipped Jesus. Apparently, Jesus also talked to his soldiers because they stopped driving, exited their vehicles, got on their knees, and started praying for forgiveness. It was beautiful. Jesus told Bashir to abandon all weapons and flags before entering the village. Instead of torturing and murdering the villagers, Jesus told them to approach humbly and offer assistance to harvest crops and build silos. All of the young men in the village had been pressed into service by militia groups, leaving only old men, women, and children.

The Lord reminded all of Bashir's men and Bashir himself that they still had free will to choose Him or reject Him. They all chose to follow Jesus. When they entered the village, they were greeted with shouting and tears of joy. One of the older ministers kissed Bashir's hand and blessed him. Everyone hugged them and fed them food that had been prepared for them. The villagers gave them clean clothes and places to bathe. Bashir and his men were smiling; they could not remember being this happy and appreciated. It was a life-changing miracle. A young boy followed Bashir everywhere and clung to his knees. Bashir found himself loving these people. After six weeks, Bashir and his men left the village to pursue other missions for Jesus.

A few of Bashir's men married young women and stayed in the village. The men had helped harvest crops and built holding structures for all the food. Everyone rejoiced and thanked the Lord Jesus. Bashir and all of his men accepted Jesus as Lord and Savior. Bashir was no longer driven by hate. He was led by the Holy Spirit. He no longer looked upon other people as inferior beings deserving to be destroyed. He realized that there is only one true God and He is the God of love. Bashir's eyes were opened because he decided to Love Jesus. Now, he knew that love was more profitable than hate, peace was preferable to war, and restoration made more sense than destruction.

Embezzle

The next time I was transported, I found myself in an upscale office building. A husband and wife owned a successful holding company, a wealth management agency that provided comprehensive, holistic advice in a broad range of financial services. They managed the portfolios of high-end clients with high-level assets.

You could almost smell the money: designer furniture, a spectacular city view, and the most aromatic smell of expensive perfume. The scent wasn't overwhelming, but rich smelling. Richard and Carolyn dressed beautifully. Richard's suit cost upward of twelve hundred dollars. Carolyn wore Prada and Louis Vuitton. They looked elegant, but their character was the opposite of their appearance. They should have been dressed in sewage-workers' uniforms.

They discussed how to embezzle millions of dollars from their wealthy clients' portfolios. They had to convince them to invest in dummy companies. Since their clients trusted them, they would not request an independent investigation of these companies. Richard and Carolyn spent months devising a scheme against their loyal customers. Although their clients were wealthy, some of them would lose almost everything. In several cases, the clients were philanthropists who gave extravagant donations to charities. The loss of their donations would be catastrophic to many needy people. Some of their clients were so fragile they might commit suicide if they suddenly found themselves indigent. Richard and Carolyn didn't care. They were already successful business partners with a legitimate practice. They were young, healthy, nice-looking people in need of nothing. Their condominium was luxurious; they had a chauffeur-driven limousine and a Lear jet. They dined at the most expensive restaurants and employed a famous chef. They flew to other countries for exotic vacations all over the world. What more could they want? More!

When they looked up from their computers, they saw me sitting at their conference table. I hardly recognized myself. I wore a St. John suit, Prada shoes, and a matching handbag. I wore genuine pearls, and my hair was perfectly coiffed; my nails were beautifully manicured. Wow, I looked great! Richard and Carolyn simultaneously said, "Who are you?" I disappeared before their eyes. Jesus began talking to them.

"Richard and Carolyn, this is Jesus. You have been blessed with youth, excellent health, and more money than you could spend in a lifetime, yet you want more. Forget about your embezzlement scheme, give your life to Me, and accept Me as your Lord and Savior. You can keep your money if you modify your lifestyle slightly. I want you to be the founders of several orphanages in different countries. Thousands of children will benefit from your generosity, and you will feel fulfilled to help others less fortunate than yourselves; however, you have free will. You must choose the path I set before you or reject Me. I want you to share your wealth. You will be blessed in so many ways. Have faith in Me."

Who wouldn't accept this invitation from Jesus Himself? Richard and Carolyn rejected Jesus. Jesus stopped talking to them. They did not feel they needed anyone, not even Jesus. The Almighty Jesus stopped talking to them and allowed them to pursue their own course. I believe pride was the first sin. Pride prevented Richard and Carolyn from becoming beloved Christians. They reminded me of the church in Laodicea in the book of Revelation where the people focused on their wealth instead of Jesus. Jesus said they were wretched, pitiful, poor, blind, and naked and that He would spew them out of His mouth. Richard and Carolyn were eventually caught and spent fifteen years in federal prison. They blamed each other for their downfall. They lost almost everything, except for money in a few offshore accounts; it was only a pittance of the wealth they used to have. Eventually, they divorced and became lonely, embittered people. Their health deteriorated while imprisoned, and they both died before their fiftieth year.

Domestic Abuse

I was transported to a house where a father, mother, and two small children sat at the kitchen table. The father was angry and spewing profanities about dinner. Although he was short in stature, he sounded like a roaring lion. I imagine, at one time, he was a nice-looking man. Now, he was bloated around the midsection, probably from consuming too much alcohol. The wife and children were too thin and pale. Although the house was clean, everything was old, washed out, and faded. The table was sturdy, but the chairs were unstable. The appliances were all old. The adjacent dining room was unfurnished. The carpeting was ragged and faded, and so were the window shades. The house smelled like mildew.

As I looked closer, I noticed the wife had a black eye and bruises on both wrists. The oldest child also had bruises on both wrists. Had they been restrained with a cord or just gripped too strongly by someone's hand? One child was seven and the other was five. They both looked stressed. The mother and the children were crying and cowering as if expecting a punch from the dad. The father was yelling at his wife because the hot dogs and spaghetti were not good enough for the amount of money he gave her for food. I was waiting for Jesus to tell me to say "Love Jesus" to the dad.

Suddenly, the wife grabbed a large kitchen knife and started cutting her husband's throat. Blood gushed everywhere. I sat there aghast. The children's screams were so loud they sounded like the siren of an emergency vehicle. The husband was limp with a confused look on his face. The scene was horrific, and the look on the wife's face was demonic. My mission was to tell the wife, "Love Jesus." After I spoke these words to her, she stopped sawing her husband's neck and calmly asked who I was. I couldn't physically intervene because I had no substance. I was a vapor, a hologram. I repeated, "Love Jesus."

Jesus began talking to Annie. "Put down the knife, Annie. You do not want your children to see you murder their father. They will be traumatized for the rest of their lives. The oldest child will eventually commit suicide, and the younger child will become a drug addict. You will spend years in prison, and you will not be able to raise your children. I know the abuse you have suffered from your husband. Come to Me right now and accept Me as your Lord and Savior. All wrongs will be made right. Your husband and children will also be saved. You will have grandchildren and great-grandchildren. Your husband will never strike you again; he will not be able to raise his voice because you severed part of his vocal cord. No charges will be pressed against you after the judge sees you and your eldest daughter. You and your family will attend church faithfully and lead many souls to Me because of your testimony."

Annie put the knife down and held a clean dishcloth over the wound. The paramedics arrived and transported her husband to the hospital, where a successful operation was performed. The girls hugged and kissed their mom. The Lord Jesus gave me a glimpse into the future twenty years later. Everyone was sitting at a new dining room table, laughing, and eating what looked like a scrumptious meal. They were celebrating many events. Annie had a degree in accounting, and the eldest daughter and her husband were both teachers and were expecting their first child. The youngest daughter had just graduated from nursing school, and the father was half-owner of the trucking company where he worked. The dad whispered a thankful blessing to Jesus for restoring their family. Everyone was so glad they decided to Love Jesus.

Active Shooter

I was transported to a small town where people attended church twice a week and believed in Biblical principles. I was standing on a rooftop next to a twenty-one-year-old young adult with an automatic assault weapon in his hand. I was startled, and it took me aback. *What in the world must have happened to cause him to be so enraged with such murderous intent?* I could sense what he was thinking. He wanted to kill at least twenty people in one day.

I said, "Love Jesus." He was astonished to see me standing beside him and asked who I was. I knew he was shaken and agitated but I repeated, "Love Jesus." I disappeared when Jesus began speaking to him. "I am Jesus, whom you have been taught about all those years in church. I know everything. I know how hypocritical your parents were at certain times; however, they did insist on you attending church and reading the Bible at home, where you learned the fundamentals of Christianity. Although you were a scholar in Sunday school, you always wanted to explore both worlds. After reading books about wizards and spells, you were fascinated by the occult. You thought they were so powerful and incredible. You taunted the neighbor's cat at age seven until he scratched you. You attempted to conjure a spell to kill him. Since he didn't die, you broke his paw. Your parents saw what you had done and sent you to counseling. That same year, you decided to begin blaming others for your misdeeds. Your friend Gloria was about to sit at the coloring table when you slipped a wad of bubble gum on her chair. She was humiliated and asked who had done it. You said that you saw Andy do it. Although Andy vehemently denied your accusation, you insisted that you saw him. Andy hated you, but you didn't care.

At ten years old, you thought it would be fun to pull the fire alarm at school. After carefully looking around to ensure no one saw you, you spotted Benjamin approaching you in the hall. He was talking on his cell phone. You pulled the alarm and blamed it on Benjamin. Although Benjamin tearfully denied it, the school investigator believed you, resulting in a month's detention for Benjamin. Benjamin told everyone that he saw you near the alarm. No one believed him.

When you were fifteen, your friend David told you he liked Felicia and asked you to set up a date for him because he was too shy to ask her out. You set up the date and told Felicia that David would come to her house, meet her parents, and take her to a movie and the ice cream parlor at five o'clock on Saturday. You told David that Felicia said she wouldn't be available on Saturday. David didn't go to Felicia's house on Saturday. Felicia was all dressed up for her first date. Her parents were livid. The following Monday, Felicia slapped David in front of everyone in the cafeteria. You laughed! When David discovered what you had done, he attempted to beat you up, but the teacher intervened. Everyone found out what you had done, and they all hated you and ostracized you the whole school year.

At seventeen, you and members of the football team went to the store after practice. Your friend Reginald bought several items and left the money on the counter, but you pocketed the money before the clerk turned around.

There was a big row between the clerk and Reginald. Fortunately, another student saw you steal the money. After that, you were booted off the team, and everybody hated you, and no one wanted to be near you. As the coach was walking down the stairs, you tripped him. He was seriously injured and had to endure several surgeries. Although you received your diploma, you were not allowed to participate in the graduation ceremony. The coach did not press charges against you.

Your parents were livid and told you what a total disappointment you had been to them your whole life and that you were the reason they never had another child. They told you that you would have probably killed your sibling or taught him or her to mimic your behavior. They told you that they wished you had never been born.

Your previous actions are why you are standing on a rooftop planning to murder twenty people because everyone has rejected you. You still have a choice. You can ask for forgiveness and be saved, or you can attempt to carry out the plan of mass murder, although it will not be successful."

I never knew what happened, but there were no reports of an active shooter who had committed mass murder from a rooftop.

The Pilot

I found myself on an airplane in the Bermuda Triangle! The pilot and copilot looked familiar; they were the same two pilots I had visited before. This time, they were visibly perplexed. I did not believe the Bermuda Triangle, or, as some call it, the Devil's Triangle, existed. The Bermuda Triangle is an airspace over the Atlantic Ocean that causes aircrafts to mysteriously disappear. One theory as to why the Bermuda Triangle exists is that the ocean's flatulence or methane gas eruptions cause disruptions in geomagnetic lines of flux. Another theory is that dangerous storms and hurricanes cause aircrafts and ships to be destroyed, or the Gulf Stream causes violent changes in the weather. Others suggest that this area is a place where a magnetic compass points toward the true north rather than the magnetic north. The Bermuda Triangle phenomenon has been studied for many years. It is an area about the size of Alaska. In 1963, the Bomber KB Hayes called the air traffic control tower complaining of engine trouble. After an exhaustive search, it was found at the bottom of the Atlantic Ocean soon after that distress call.

Five airplanes disappeared on December 5, 1945. These five planes were known as Flight 19. The plane searching for Flight 19 also vanished over the same area. Imagine not being able to rely on your compass and other instruments, such as your altimeter. Thick clouds enveloping the aircraft make it impossible for the pilots to rely on their vision. Sometimes, the pilots experience vertigo and become disoriented.

In 1482, Columbus sailed in this area and recorded seeing flames on the sea. It was later discovered that Bermuda was formed from volcanic explosions; unusual lava covered the island. This lava had high amounts of titanium oxide, iron oxide, and magnetite.

More magnetite is in Bermuda than anywhere else in the world. Recently, pilots have relied on GPS and no longer fear the Bermuda Triangle.

The captain began talking to his copilot, telling him that he was concerned about not clearing the storm because they had used an exorbitant amount of fuel, and the GPS was erratic, not telling the altitude or location. He could not reach the tower.

I said, "Love Jesus." The captain was startled. Years before, he had heard those exact words but hadn't seen anyone. Now he looked directly at me, standing there in my flight attendant uniform. He asked who I was. His copilot also heard me and saw me. The pilot said it was déjà vu. I disappeared before their eyes. Jesus started talking to the captain.

"Edwin, this is Jesus. Although you have never accepted Me as your Lord and Savior, you know about Me. Your family took you to church every week, but when you became an adult, you stopped attending church with your wife and children. You abandoned the ministries you had joined and started meeting that young flight attendant at a hotel every chance you could sneak away. You fell madly in love with her. You started spending less time with your family and stopped attending church altogether. What happened to your moral principles?

Edwin, you have to make a life choice whether to continue on the path you are pursuing or to repent and accept My free offer of salvation. Whether you accept Me or not, you will find your way out of the storm. Think about what would happen if you crashed and died in this Bermuda Triangle. Your soul would be lost, and you would spend an eternity in Hell. Your wife would find out about your affair. She already suspects there is another woman. Your wife and children would not remember you fondly. My desire for you is that you allow Me to rescue you from a wretched life of deceit, infidelity, and lies. I want you to tell others about Me, beginning with your copilot. Rekindle the love you once had for your family. The teen ministry needs a teacher. Choose Me and choose a fulfilled Christian life."

Edwin began crying uncontrollably as he found a path out of the Bermuda Triangle. He could see an opening in the clouds. The co-pilot was silent, trying to digest all that had happened. After the plane landed safely, all the passengers applauded the captains, grateful for a successful landing. Edwin praised God and asked for forgiveness. Edwin gave God all the glory. I believe Edwin decided to Love Jesus.

Assassination

Next, I was transported to India. I was standing in the royal palace; the furniture was plush and very beautiful. The captain of the palace security force was talking to a foreigner with an Eastern European accent or maybe Russian. At first, the Indian man was protesting vehemently, his voice raised to fever pitch. The Eastern European man showed him a picture on his cell phone. The demeanor of the Indian man changed instantly. The Indian man's name was Aarush. When he looked at the cellphone, he saw his mother, his wife, and children sitting on a sofa in his home, while being held captive at gunpoint by two burly Russian-looking men. His family looked terrified!

The Russian man's name was Ludvic. He told Aarush that unless he received the exact location and the time the Prime Minister would be on stage, Aarush's family would be killed. Aarush said nothing as Ludvic left the room, reminding Aarush that he had one-half hour to comply. Aarush broke down crying because he knew that if the Prime Minister were assassinated, his country would no longer be a democracy. Should he consider his family's well-being above preserving freedom for his country that he had sworn to protect at all costs? Were his family's lives more important than those of all the other families in his country?

Aarush was a Buddhist who believed that human suffering was the way to achieve nirvana: peace, salvation, and enlightenment. Apparently, he failed as a Buddhist because all he felt was anxiety and confusion. He knew he could pray to Buddha, but the only answer he would possibly receive was a feeling of peace. He needed an honest answer to his dilemma.

I said, "Love Jesus." Aarush looked around and saw me. He shook his head in disbelief. I was dressed in a beautiful long silk saree, and my appearance was enhanced with an upswept hairstyle. I had on real jewelry and beautiful silken slippers. Wow! Arush asked if I were his reincarnated grandmother or his dead aunt. I just stood there, looked at him, and repeated, "Love Jesus." After that, I disappeared.

Jesus began talking to Aarush. "Aarush, I am Jesus, the Son of the living God who loved you enough to die on the Cross for your sin and everyone's sins. I will help you if you will pray to Me and ask Me to be the Lord of your life. There is no other God, declaring the end from the beginning and from ancient times things that are not yet done; saying, I will do My pleasure and My counsel will stand. I was there when your father died of a heart attack while working on the family farm. I watched as your mother gave birth to you in that makeshift hospital. I healed you because you were born with a defective heart. The doctors at the main hospital said it was a miracle you survived. "

Aarush fell to the ground and lay prostrate, worshipping Jesus. He asked for forgiveness for all his sins and for Jesus to intercede for him because he did not know what to do. Jesus told Aarush to warn the Prime Minister of the assassination plot. Jesus told Aarush that He would cause the two assassins to leave Aarush's house before they could kill his family. Jesus told Aarush that he must have faith. Aarush trusted Jesus. Aarush's wife called to tell him that the two men had gone after receiving an urgent call. Jesus caused the men to hear static over their telephone, thinking Ludvic needed them to vacate the premises before the police arrived.

Aarush phoned the state police to arrest Ludvic and his accomplices. Aarush was promoted; however, he did not inform people that he had become a Christian. A few months later, he shared with everyone what had happened and proclaimed that Jesus Christ is the King of Kings and the Lord of Lords.

Bus Driver

The next time I was transported, I found myself on a school bus. I was dressed in an expensive Vicuna wool blazer and skirt, Louis Vuitton loafers, and carrying a matching handbag. The children wore the same uniform, only with Stuart Weisman loafers. *Who were these rich kids? Why were they riding on a school bus instead of a chauffeured limousine?*

I discovered that riding a school bus would make them feel more on par with ordinary children their age. These children were so quiet it was eerie; they barely spoke above a whisper. Their noses were in the air. Their heads were held so high I wondered to whom I was to say, "Love Jesus." As I glanced toward the bus driver, I knew he was the person to whom I was to speak.

He looked ordinary in his bus driver's uniform, being of average height and weight for a forty-year-old man. He looked disgruntled and disgusted with life. When the last child exited the bus, he started talking aloud. He hadn't noticed me yet. He said, "Good riddance to rich rubbish. I am glad to be rid of you privileged, snotty brats. I loathe and despise every one of you and your parents and your teachers. You have no manners and are rude, crude, and obnoxious."

I noticed that none of the children said goodbye or thank you as they exited the bus. They didn't even look in his direction. Phillip Goodman finished his shift, returned to the bus barn, and socialized with his colleagues in the break room.

While discussing their day, they drank coffee and soft drinks. All the drivers agreed that the snobby rich kids were the worst. Phillip told them how a parent had accused him of stealing their daughter's gold pendant only to find it later at her home. The parent never apologized to him. On another occasion, he was accused of fondling a little girl when he attempted to prevent her from falling down the school bus steps. Phillip said he grabbed both of her shoulders. Fortunately, the owner of the bus company did not believe the parents. The owner was accustomed to hearing unfounded accusations from the richy rich.

According to the other bus drivers, the kids from the orphanage were friendly and happy. They baked cookies and gave them to the drivers. Handmade birthday cards and Christmas cards were often given to the drivers. Children from middle schools who had working-class parents were delightful. Although they were loud, singing and laughing, they were very respectful. The company had a rotating policy where every driver had to drive all three routes. Phillip was the newest employee, so he had no choice as to which group of children he had to drive first. Phillip had to drive the rich children for a semester, everyone's least favorite route. After Phillip had been employed for a year, he realized that the rich kids were the only ones he disliked.

At the end of Phillip's shift, the parents of two children who rode his bus and Phillip's boss were waiting for him. The parent said that her two daughters saw Phillip kissing and having sex with the young bus attendant after the children exited the bus. Actually, Phillip and the bus attendant had shared a bagged lunch, laughed, and talked. These two girls had blatantly lied, and what made matters worse was that the boss looked at Phillip as if he were guilty! His boss reprimanded Phillip verbally in front of the parents, the children, and his coworkers. Phillip's boss told him that his behavior was reprehensible and inappropriate and that he would be fired if there were any more complaints.

Phillip was livid. "I will wipe the smirks off their faces." An evil thought is Satan's opportunity. As Phillip was driving over a bridge, a truck hit the school bus from behind because the truck driver was not paying attention. The truck hit the bus again before Phillip could maneuver and escape from falling over the railing. The two front wheels of the bus were dangling over the guard- rails.

Phillip started thinking, I could have the kids move to the rear and put the bus in reverse, simultaneously stepping on the gas pedal. We could all be saved because the front wheels would come down from the rail, or I could keep the bus in gear and cause the bus to tip over into the lake, thus killing all of us.

I really don't have any reason to live. Knowing that I caused these rich kids and their parents to suffer would be gratifying. I despise all of them: the children, the parents, and the administrators. I think that is what I will do.

Phillip looked through his mirror and saw me standing there. While everyone else was screaming, I calmly walked to the front of the bus. I said, "Love Jesus." Phillip asked who I was and why I wasn't upset. I disappeared before his face, and Jesus began talking to him. "Phillip, I am Jesus. I realize you are unhappy, disappointed, and angry because you feel your life has not progressed the way you thought. People lied about you but remember that people lied about Me and crucified Me even though I never sinned. I willingly died so all humanity could be saved. It is not too late for you to live a wonderful, fulfilled life serving Me and your community. Do not kill yourself and all of these innocent children. Confess your sins, earnestly repent, and accept the free gift of salvation through Me. Seek Me while I may be found and call on Me while I am near. Let the wicked forsake his ways and the unrighteous man his thoughts. Let him return to Me, and I will abundantly pardon. These children have potential, and many of them will accept Me as their Lord and Savior. Give them and yourself the opportunity for salvation."

Tears wet the front of Phillip's shirt as he cried profusely. Phillip realized that Jesus is real and accepting Him was the right decision. Phillip asked Jesus to forgive him for all of his sins, past, present, and future. Phillip turned the bus's wheels and instructed the children to come to the front. The bus was teetering over the guard rail. God gave Phillip a different strategy from what he had previously contemplated. Philip told all the children to stomp as hard as they could. The wheels jumped over the guard rails as Phillip pressed hard on the accelerator. Phillip remained calm because he knew that Jesus would rescue them. Phillips' strategy worked because all wheels were back on the highway.

The children, the spectators, the people from the news media, the parents, and the school administrators all clapped their hands and cheered for Phillip. They all chanted, "Mr. P, you are the man!" When the children exited the bus into their loving parents' arms, they hugged Phillip around the neck and thanked him. The policemen, firefighters, and other bus drivers all shook his hand. Phillip stopped them from praising him and told them that they should thank Jesus for giving him the strategy to maneuver the bus successfully. Everyone who knew him was shocked because they never heard him mention Jesus. Phillip's favorite route is now the rich kids' route. They say good morning and good afternoon and they bring him gifts that they made in arts and craft classes. Phillip is invited to their birthday parties. Phillip leads a youth ministry in his church and teaches Bible lessons to his friends in the bus barn social room. Phillip is so glad that he decided to Love Jesus.

Street Gang

The next time I was transported, I found myself in a familiar landscape: an alley in my neighborhood where I saw four gang members and a victim named James. Marcellus, the gang leader, explained to James why he had to murder him. James, a recent college graduate who returned to the neighborhood after his father died and his mother suffered a stroke, stood there looking horrified.

James had testified against Marcellus' brother fifteen years earlier. Marcellus' brother,

Richard, had chosen James' brother, Ray, as a "menu item" to kill for his gang initiation ultimatum. How depraved is having to kill someone to belong to a gang? James was an eyewitness to his brother's assassination. James was attempting to explain about his mother's stroke and the reason he had to return to the neighborhood.

I interrupted James and said to Marcellus, "Love Jesus." Marcellus looked around, saw me, and said, "Who the Hell are you?" I was dressed in an expensive Gucci athletic outfit and Timberland boots. I repeated, "Love Jesus." Apparently, everyone heard me because they all repeated, "Love Jesus?" A quizzical expression was on all their faces. I disappeared before their faces. There was a tense silence. Jesus began speaking to Marcellus.

"Marcellus, this is Jesus. Do you remember when your older brother had to choose someone to murder as an initiation to join the street gang that you now lead? Ray and his family were working in their front yard when your brother shot Ray three times in the heart. His brother James was standing near him and saw everything; his parents' heads were turned. James testified against your brother. Threats from your gang caused James to leave home and live with his grandmother in another state. When his father died, he had no choice but to return home to care for his bedridden mother. If you kill him, what will happen to his mother? Marcellus, you have a choice: love Me and walk away, or have your crew kill James. If you kill James, all of you will live a wretched life of crime with many sorrows. Choose Me and choose life, freedom, a future, and hope. You are the leader; they will blindly follow you."

Looking tranquil and expectant, Marcellus apologized to James and said no one would harm him anymore. Marcellus and his posse decided to follow Jesus and not continue a life of crime anymore. Everyone walked home quietly while looking around to see where I had gone. They all knew they had witnessed a supernatural event.

Prison Guard

The next time I was transported, I found myself in a prison. I watched as a sadistic guard named Lampkin brutalized the prisoners. Listening to the prisoners informed me about Lampkin before I actually observed the abuse. He performed a depraved ritual every night. Waking his prey after midnight, he would handcuff them and shackle their ankles. He would take them to his office and beat them until his fists bled. Often, he would beat them with a baton. Everyone was too afraid to report him. His hateful, demonic, mean behavior should not have been tolerated, but it was because even his superiors feared him. I was surprised that the prisoners did not conspire to stop him. None of the prisoners ever attempted to defend themselves; they were petrified with fear.

One night, Lampkin chose Luke to become his latest victim. After so many conquests without any real resistance, Lampkin underestimated the strength and agility of Luke. When Lampkin woke Luke, Luke began to scream because he was so startled. He never dreamed Lampkin would attempt to accost him because of his size. Luke was six feet, six inches tall and weighed two hundred and sixty pounds. He was all muscle. Lampkin had already handcuffed him and was attempting to gag his mouth. Luke struggled as Lampkin tried to put shackles on his ankles. Luke only had two more days to be incarcerated because the judge had decided to dismiss the charges against him. A robber had attempted to take Luke's car keys and wallet at gunpoint. Being an ex-Marine, Luke fought back and injured the robber severely. Luke should not have been arrested in the first place. A public defender finally convinced the judge to drop the charges after reading the lengthy rap sheet of the robber. Lampkin struggled to get Luke back to his office. Luke used his unshackled feet to trip Lampkin, and he managed to get Lampkin in a chokehold. Although Luke was handcuffed, he was about to choke Lampkin to death. I am ashamed to say that I did not feel sorry for Lampkin. I quickly repented. I appeared just as Lampkin was turning blue. I was dressed in a prison guard's uniform and said, "Love Jesus. '

Luke stopped choking Lampkin and looked at me as if he expected me to shoot him or beat him with a baton. There was nothing in my hands. I just repeated, "Love Jesus."

"Who are you, and what do you mean, Love Jesus?" I disappeared right before his eyes. Jesus began speaking to both of them. This was a first for me. "Luke, this is Jesus speaking to you. Although this murder would be self-defense, you would have to serve some jail time. Eventually, you would be killed by another inmate for bragging rights. An inmate would say that he killed the person who took down Lampkin. Now, he would be the most feared prisoner. Your present sentence will be over in two short days, and you will be a free man returning to your family and job. Accept Me as your Lord and Savior and live a long, productive life as a Christian."

Lampkin had begun to regain consciousness when Jesus began talking to him. Jesus told Lampkin that because he had chosen to always listen to Satan instead of Him, his family had him institutionalized because they feared him. Jesus told Lampkin that he had a choice if Luke decided to let him live. He could choose Jesus and live a saved life, becoming a person who respected everyone, including prisoners. He would become a prisoner rights advocate and fight for prison reform. Reporting Luke would result in Luke's serving another month, but Lampkin would be fired and charged with several crimes against inmates. The state prison system would be sued for millions of dollars. Luke would be killed in prison, and it would be Lampkin's fault. Jesus told Lampkin that he would become homeless and consider suicide. Jesus told them that both of them had free will. They could choose Him who is life, or they could choose to reject Him, thus choosing death. I was not allowed to see what happened. I pray that both of them chose Jesus.

Re-education Camp

I thought I had been transported to Hell when I saw what was happening to people. A re-education camp is what this facility was called. Brutal guards were torturing people, sometimes entire families. People were being cut with machetes and sharp knives. Hot oil was poured on a man's hand to observe the burn pattern. *Was this Nazi Germany?* The administrator, Chang, was especially cruel. He was supervising the murder of a family of five at the hands of their teenage daughter. Her family members wore hangman hoods over their heads, but she knew exactly who they were. Chang told her to shoot each of them in the head, and if she refused, he would order ten sadistic soldiers to sexually violate her until she died. She would not be allowed to die until she watched her entire family cut to pieces with machetes. Her cries for mercy were heart-wrenching, but to no avail. Chang finally convinced her that the more humane death for her family was to be shot rather than the alternative. The young girl pleaded with Chang, but he just sneered at her and struck her in the face so hard that she fell to the floor, howling in pain as several of her teeth fell to the ground.

I startled Chang when I walked right up to him. I was in his face. Enraged and indignant would be the adjectives to describe his countenance. He ordered his soldiers to cut my head off. Three men approached me with drawn swords and attempted to decapitate me. I have no substance, so their attempts were futile. Jesus told me that now was the time to say, "Love Jesus." I shouted in a booming voice, "Love Jesus!" My voice sounded amplified, as if I were speaking into a microphone. Several soldiers ran toward me and attempted to cut me, but their weapons went through the air, unable to penetrate my holographic image. There was hush and awe. Everyone stared at me; I looked ordinary because I was dressed in prison garb. Silence and confusion followed.

Jesus did something spectacular. He addressed everyone Himself. "I am Jesus who came in the flesh to be crucified for your sins. I was born of a virgin and preached for three years on the earth. It is my desire that all people would be saved. After evil men crucified me, I arose on the third day. I am alive. This regime will cease to exist. All of you have an opportunity to live in a democratic society or to die and go to Hell, a real place for people who do not sincerely repent. Enough is enough. People who desire to continue torturing and killing have a choice right now. You cannot deceive Me because I know your hearts. Since none of you have read the Bible, you don't know the story of Moses. A rebellious group of people chose to challenge my choice for a leader. I caused the ground to open up and swallow them alive. The rest of their advocates were consumed with fire. Brutality and lawlessness will end now in your Godless country. All who oppose my decision to give you a democratic society will die and be eternally lost because I know your heart. Let Me be perfectly clear. Choosing to live in a democratic society does not mean that you are saved. You must choose Me as your Lord and Savior. You will have free will to choose Me or reject Me. Being a loving and kind person in your new society will not save your soul; you must choose salvation through Me by making Me the Lord of your life. "

Would you believe that not everyone chose to live in freedom? About eighty-five percent of the people bowed their knees and prayed to Jesus, thanking him for an opportunity to live free. All prisoners walked out of their cells and torture chambers. The prisoners who were in critical condition were miraculously healed! Millions of people gathered in the town square. Messiah Jesus extended the invitation again to live a better life in a free society. Several rulers, soldiers, and even oppressed citizens rejected Jesus's offer. The Supreme Leader and his family were the most defiant as they stood at the entrance to their opulent palace.

Suddenly, there was screaming and wailing when people realized what was happening. The people who rejected Jesus were swallowed when the ground opened beneath their feet. The millions of people with clean hearts cried tears of joy for their deliverance from an oppressive, demonic government.

About the Author

Katherine Michelle Woods is a retired elementary educator who believes faith in God can transform troubled lives. As society becomes more technologically advanced, belief in God has dwindled. Therefore, Ms. Woods is committed to publishing books highlighting that God is still granting miracles.